ELEPHANT ME

GILES ANDREAE

GUY PARKER-REES

ORCHARD

Elephant Mighty reclined on his throne
At the start of the Elephant Games.
"Impress me," he said to the little ones there,
"And I'll give you your ELEPHANT NAMES."

Tradition dictated, in elephant lore,
That **ALL** of the young ones compete
To try to be better than everyone else
At a certain spectacular feat.

And each time an elephant managed to prove
A talent or skill to the king,
The monarch would give him his **ELEPHANT NAME**…
An honour they all longed to win.

Nina was first to try out for a name;
The largest young elephant there.
She pulled a whole tree from the ground by its roots
And lifted it high in the air.

"AMAZING!" cried Elephant Mighty. "Hoorah!
Your trunk is so splendid and long!
I never imagined that tree would come loose.
I'm calling you **ELEPHANT STRONG!**"

Young Norcus was next, so he took a deep breath
And, summoning all of his might,
He let out a bellow so loud and so shrill
That even the vultures took flight.

"REMARKABLE!" Elephant Mighty declared.
"That sound, it could set off a riot!
I'm calling you **ELEPHANT NOISY**, my boy.
Now, shush! Settle down and be quiet!"

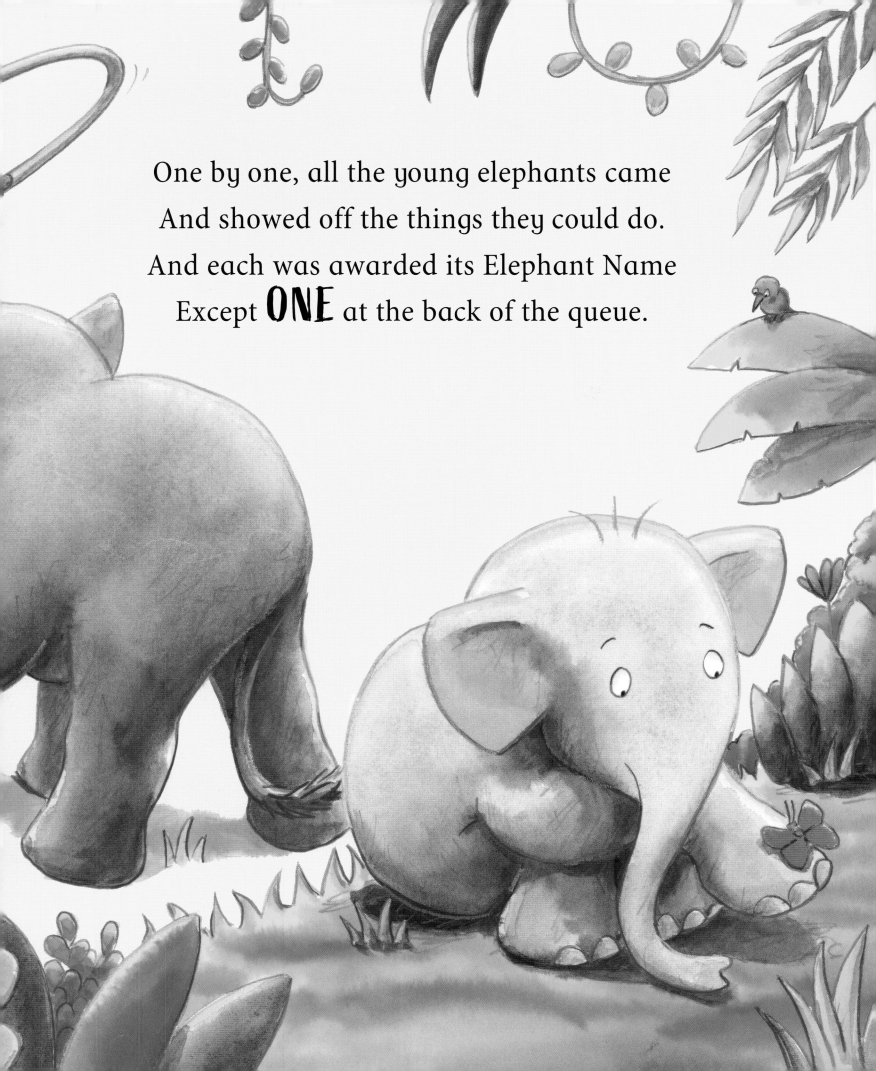

One by one, all the young elephants came
And showed off the things they could do.
And each was awarded its Elephant Name
Except **ONE** at the back of the queue.

"I see one more elephant hiding away.
Come, show yourself now," said the king.
"Yes, tell me what marvellous trick you can do.
Please demonstrate – what is your thing?"

"I'm not really sure yet,
Your Highness," he said.
"It's just that . . . I don't
really know."

"Oh nonsense," said
Elephant Mighty, "what tosh!
Get on with it.
Give me a show!"

So Num-Num stepped forward
and did a few tricks.

He was trying as
hard as he could,

But Elephant Mighty
was most unimpressed
Asking, "Can't you do
anything good?"

"Oh dear," scowled the king. "No, that really won't do."
Poor Num-Num felt hopelessly small.
"I should call you **ELEPHANT NOTHING**," he laughed.
"Yes, **ELEPHANT NOTHING-AT-ALL!**"

So Num-Num decided to move far away,
To a place where no elephants go.
He trudged through the dust and the heat of the plains,
His head and his tail hanging low.

But soon, because Num-Num was **GENTLE** and **KIND**,
And was blessed with a **GENEROUS SOUL**,
Lions and zebra, giraffes and gazelle
Came and shared his new watering hole.

Then one day, a warthog asked, "Why are you here?"
So Num-Num explained what occurred.
"That's nonsense!" a crocodile swiftly replied,
And his friends all agreed, "That's absurd!"

"You're good at all sorts of things. Really, you are!
You're **FRIENDLY**, you're **KIND**, and you're **TRUE**.
Out of all of the animals here on these plains,
There's only one . . . only one **YOU!**"

"Come, follow me, Num-Num," the crocodile said.
"Let's take you back where you belong,
And tell Mr Elephant Thingumy-jig
That he's not only foolish, but wrong!"

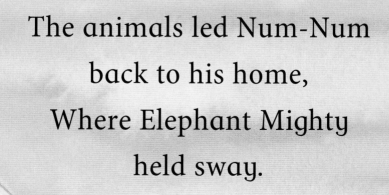

The animals led Num-Num
back to his home,
Where Elephant Mighty
held sway.

"Excuse me, Your Highness," said Num-Num, "it's me,
And this time I've got something to say."
He cleared his throat nervously, took a deep breath,
Then looked up, as brave as can be.

"I'll tell you my Elephant Name," Num-Num said,

"I want to be

ELEPHANT
ME."

"You want to be **ELEPHANT ME?**" sneered the king,
With a haughty and arrogant snort.
"There's nothing about it that says what you **DO**.
That's a really **RIDICULOUS** thought!"

"It's not," Num-Num said, "because that's who I am.
I may not be noisy or tough,
But the hardest thing sometimes is just to be **YOU**,
And to know being **YOU** is **ENOUGH**."

To all of the creatures' astonished surprise,
The king didn't bellow or shout.
No, Elephant Mighty had started to **WEEP**,
And a long, lonely wail came out.

"You're right," cried the monarch, "it's hard to be YOU. And guess what? It's hard to be ME! I'm tired being Elephant Mighty all day. I want to be ELEPHANT FREE!"

"I'm longing to do all those things that I can't . . .
That a king's not expected to do,
Like **DANCING** all night beneath only the stars,
With my feet getting wet in the dew!

Who cares about all these ridiculous names?
No, what's more important by far,
Is just to be true to ourselves every day,
And content with . . .

WHOEVER WE ARE."

"**ELEPHANT ME!** What a wonderful thing!
Now, whenever we see there's a chance,
Let's celebrate **ME-NESS** with all of our hearts,

And right now, I see stars . . .